A KNIFE FOR MY LOVE

Steve Page has a little problem. His beautiful wife Archie is disenchanted with his business prospects, and decides that she wants a better life than he can offer her. His boss, Lou Honnicutt, represents for her the next rung up the earnings ladder; and Honnicutt is willing to marry her if she'll divorce Steve. But Steve actually loves his wife dearly. His problem is: how to keep her. He decides that "A KNIFE FOR MY LOVE" is the only answer.

Here are ten gripping tales wrenched from the pages of the 1950s and '60s pulp magazines—hardboiled stories of the bad men and bad girls that haunt the urban and suburban byways of American big-city life. They'll keep you gasping for more!

Borgo Press Books by MORRIS HERSHMAN/LIONEL WEBB

A KNIFE FOR MY LOVE

AND FURTHER MAYHEM

MORRIS HERSHMAN

THE BORGO PRESS

MMXIII

A KNIFE FOR MY LOVE

FIRST EDITION

Published by Wildside Press LLC

www.wildsidebooks.com

A KNIFE FOR MY LOVE

CONTENTS

THE BATTERED BRIDE

Gilman walked down the street as if he were on honest business. At a glassed-in phone booth near the corner he paused, then walked in and dialed swiftly.

"Fredrics? I'm all set."

The man on the other end of the line sounded anxious. "That's definite. I suppose? You are going through with it?"

"Definitely."

"It's pretty dangerous, you know," Jim Fredrics told him. "Don't let yourself get seen—except by one person."

Gilman hung up and left the booth. He walked past the end of town to the spot where he had parked, drove to a white-painted, three-story house half a mile away.

He got out and walked along a flagstone path, glancing at a badminton court close to him and at a swimming pool. He picked up a sunflower and squeezed its stem till the juice was spread over his palm.

After he touched the bulge in his side pocket, he knocked at the door.

His knock was answered by a blonde in a flower-patterned bathrobe and white mules. She could still have passed for eighteen, Gilman thought, married and all; and he wished his heart didn't beat faster at the sight of her.

"Get dressed, Renée," he snapped. "You're coming with me."

"Why—what is it, Tom? My husb—"

"He's never home till five o'clock and for now you're with me," Gilman said, reaching in his pocket and showing the ugly black snout of a Colt Cobra. "Get dressed."

"I never thought you'd do a thing like this, Tom. You always seemed like not a bad guy."

She dressed quickly, tearing a stocking in the process. With sweat-soaked fingers she eased herself into spotted white slacks and finally fumbled a white shirt and jacket onto herself.

Gilman had been glancing around at the expensive furniture. A smile tugged at his lips. "You're doing all right, even if your husband *is* out of the rackets," he said.

"My husband will never again hang around with people he knows are the dregs of—"

Gilman raised the colt Cobra as if to smash it across Renée's mouth, but couldn't bring himself to do it. Too damn good-hearted, that was his trouble, he told himself grimly.

Renée walked first, gesturing idly with the house keys. Gilman told her to put them away. Nobody saw him with her on the way to the car. He drove swiftly, smelling grass that bent to the wind on both sides of him.

"I used to like you, Tom," Renée said softly as Gilman stopped the car in a grove of trees. "If you'd gotten out of the rackets first—"

"Forget it," he growled, and kept from saying that he had always like her and still did, in a way.

He turned to her as she sat framed against the scenery of gray rock cliff shining in the sun. "Here's where I go to work on you," he said.

The girl fell back in terror against the door. As he raised a fist she suddenly opened the door, nearly dropping against it. She fell out of the car at last, losing her balance completely. As Gilman started to leave by the opened door, she reached up hurriedly and slammed it shut, hoping for precious seconds to get her faculties together.

Gilman backed up the car and turned it around so that he was facing her. Wide-eyed, the girl turned to run. Gilman followed her iin thue car, a cat playing with a mouse. The girl glanced back over a shoulder to see that the car was lumbering along after her.

She swerved, then, finally running toward the gray-faced cliff that offered her the one chance of safety. Gilman gunned the car.

For a time, scrambling over the rocks with the animal speed that fear had given her, she seemed to have actually outdistanced him. It was less her lack of speed than a hidden, moss-covered rock that made her fall heavily, twisting hard as she landed, so that the rock, which could have crushed her chest cavity, glanced off her ribs.

She cried out then, but miraculously regained her feet, stumbling drunkenly toward the rock face, so near and yet so terribly far.

It was close, but Renée reached the cliff. Gilman cursed loudly, then drew out the Colt Cobra. He fired once, and watched his bullet chip a piece of gray rock out of the cliff.

Renée, throwing fear-filled glances back of her, scrambled up the cliff toward a place where a huge rock lay on a wide ledge. The rock would give cover.

She stiffened when Gilman fired again, then fell. Gilman didn't go up to the cliff after her, but drove away from the scene as quickly as he could.

There was a phone booth in the first gas station he reached, and Gilman called his pal Jim Fredrics from there.

"I took care of Renée," he said. "I fired over her head twice when I'd got her away from the house, and she was smart enough to play possum. I guess she'll not get home for a few more hours at least. What happened at the other end?"

"You mean about the boys?" Fredrics asked. "They did it. Got to the house at five o'clock, just when Renée's husband got home, and chopped him to pieces for thinking he could get out of the rackets. One thing the boss always hates, and that's a quitter."

"I know," Gilman said, thinking of Renée. "Or else I might have been the first one to—well, never mind. I suppose the guy is dead."

"You suppose exactly right," Fredrics told him. "All according to plan. And if you hadn't gotten Renée out of the house in time, she'd have been killed for knowing too much about how her husband got it."

"It's almost a shame she'll always think of me as a sore boyfriend and not a guy who kept her out of trouble and saved her life."

"I was wondering," Fredrics asked. "What made you do it?"

"Well. I've always liked Renée and I still do," Gilman said. "Do you know what's the trouble with me, Jim? I'm too good-natured, that's all."

CHARLOTTE'S RUSE

"Of course it's no crime to apply for non-service of jury duty if you have some honest reason," Ms. Driscoll looked toward the right side of her desk through soft gray eyes warm with sympathy. "The City doesn't pay me to put someone on a jury panel who shouldn't be there."

Mr. Junius Brutus Egmont nodded brusquely at those first words, but paid no attention to the others as he rooted busily inside a leather briefcase.

"This here ought to do the trick," he snapped.

The letter, on a local dentist's stiff white stationery, insisted that Mr. J. B. Egmont was having root canal work done on four teeth, so he ought to be excused from jury duty. Convincing enough, but a significant contradiction appeared under the dentist's address.

"He also works on two nights a week, so he'd be able to see you then," she pointed out, not quite so sympathetic this time. "You have to give me a valid reason to excuse you."

"I'm always prepared, believe it." Egmont looked like an experienced swimmer ready for the waters of modern bureaucracy. "This letter will cut it for sure."

"Apparently you have back trouble, too, and can't sit for long." Charlotte Driscoll's eyes narrowed as she put this letter down flat on her desk. "We can still use you on cases that won't take too long to hear."

"You—*this* is a pain in the—okay! Thought I'd lost this, which is the only reason I brought the other two with me."

"This letter if from your employer at the Brickell Medical Supply Company here in the city. It says you're needed on your job."

"I've been the firm's best salesman for eight years, and some important deals are due to come up very soon."

Charlotte Driscoll suddenly stood. "Back in a minute." She hurried to a desk at the far end of the room. After speaking with a colleague, she picked up his phone.

The two letters that hadn't been returned to Egmont weren't on the desk. That woman must have taken them. He didn't particularly need them now, but they belonged to him and he'd had to sweat before getting them. His eyes were still glinting angrily under thick glasses when she walked back to her place.

"I want my letters back before I go," he said, looking at her empty hands. "I went to the trouble of getting them."

"They'll be evidence," Charlotte Driscoll said bluntly. "They'll help to show that you broke into different offices when equipment was stolen."

"What are you talking about?"

"You showed more letters than anybody was likely to have, and a co-worker of mine agreed with my suspicion that two of them had been typed on the same machine. I phoned the police to find out if there'd been complaints about stationery taken from those three offices. The answer was yes. It had been removed during a long series of full-scale burglaries with plenty of medical equipment stolen from many offices as well."

"What the hell! I'm getting out before you claim I attacked you or something." Egmont was standing as a policeman hurried over.

"You did make your point with all those letters, and you won't serve on any jury," Charlotte Driscoll said. "But you'll see a short trial very soon now, and you'll be the defendant."

"I can bring plenty of letters from my psychiatrists to say I'm not responsible for whatever happened," Egmont said exultantly, and Charlotte Driscoll blanched.

CHICKEN CONTEST

Larry Reitz could sense that it was building up, and that there was no way to stop it. He stood under the lamppost and listened as Skeets Carty growled out: "Chicken talk, that's all! The yellow is running out from your collar!"

Phil said grimly, "I'll do anything you will."

"That's a deal, punk." Skeets was solemn. He hitched up his pants and gave an unpleasant grin, showing his yellow teeth. "You've always been scared of heights."

It was time for Larry to interfere. He said urgently, "Let's not do anything we'll be sorry for. You know the way Phil feels about heights."

Phil Kramer swore under his breath. A couple of years ago, his father had climbed out on a window ledge in their top floor tenement apartment, and kept the cop emergency squads at bay for over an hour. Then he had jumped off.

Phil said, tight-lipped, "what is it you have in mind. Name it."

"Well, we can do a little something I learned about up at the Big Place."

Skeets smiled when he referred to the State

Reformatory. But he didn't feel like smiling. Just remembering what the Royal Purples had been saying about his girl made him feel like crippling Phil for life. Hoodlum rumor had gone out that Peggy had been two-timing him with Phil while he had been sweating out his term in a big wooden barracks with young punks he wouldn't have spoken to twice outside.

"We'll do this," Skeets said grimly. "We go up to a height and then jump off. What's the matter? You look scared."

"Who do you think you're kidding." Phil swallowed. But he looked sick under the lamplight's harsh white glow. "Name a place you want us to jump off."

"The Narrows."

Phil Kramer drew in a shocked breath. "Wait now, look—you don't mean that!"

"Sure I do." Skeets Carty was grinning. "It ain't more than a couple hundred feet down into the river. If anything happens to one of us—well, that's how the breaks go."

Phil started to say something, but he kept his lips tight together instead, and turned to Larry.

"I'll be the ref," Larry said slowly. "Let's get a move on."

The three of them walked slowly along the ill-lit streets. Larry Reitz was first and the other two stayed well back of him and some ten feet from each other. When Larry suddenly glanced back, he saw Skeets looking contemptuously toward Phil and Phil sticking out his chin as he walked.

Skeets called out sharply, "What are you two crawling for?"

"We're practically there, Skeets," Larry answered quickly. "Don't you remember the way? It hasn't been so long that you'd forget it."

The Narrows, as the bridge was called, wasn't very long. There was a path at each side for people who'd want to walk across. The metal rails were smooth surfaces broken up by a series of knob-like projections, each coming to a point. Every ninth knob had been replaced by a lamppost which wasn't usually lighted.

"The bridge looks crummier than it used to," Skeets snarled, his voice growing a little ghostly in the soft wind. "Okay, we can do it here. Right at this here place we can get started. All clear down below."

"There are no cars coming, and I don't see a sign of anybody watching," Larry said.

Skeets said, turning to Phil Kramer, "How you feeling, punk?"

"Never felt better!" Phil answered after a pause. "It used to be a lot colder here."

"Maybe you're feeling kind of warm and that makes the whole difference." Skeets Carty threw back his big head and laughed. When he was serious again, he said, "We'll do it together."

"Why not? That suits me fine." Sweat drops showed dully on Phil Kramer's face.

"Okay, let's climb."

Carefully, Skeets lifted a foot into a circular cavity in the metalwork and, holding onto a knob, he sat down on the rail. Still holding the knob, he straightened himself and stepped down to a ledge so narrow he stood on tiptoes.

"How about his, huh? I must be looking like your old man when he knocked himself off. Get out here, Phil."

Phil Kramer was very slow about it, his breath coming hard. His eyes bulged as his hands gripped one of the pointed knobs. He called out when he felt Skeets half-touching, half-pushing him.

"So far, so good," Skeets said. "Now turn around so you can look out. You can't see no water, but turn, anyhow."

It took Phil a minute. Then Larry Reitz, standing back of the rail, said quietly, "I'll count to five, then you both jump. One, two, three, four—"

In the pause, Skeets Carty said disgustedly, "Who needs a count!" One minute he was on the ledge, the next minute his body whistled through the night.

Phil shuddered, then turned as best he could and climbed back up the rail until he was next to Larry Reitz on the bridge.

He said quietly, "Skeets was away for such a long time he didn't know that the city was draining the river at this point to put up a new housing project."

The only answer was the sound of a sickening thud below, which was followed by silence.

THE DEVIL'S PAYOFF

Stephen Sherdell had always believed that honesty paid very poor dividends and it was perhaps only a fear of the law which had prevented him from putting that conviction to the test. But a fear can be completely out-weighed by circumstances of an unusual nature.

It started when he saw the man in the rumpled suit come into the bank one afternoon. The newcomer walked over to the cage closest to Sherdell and pushed across to the teller what looked like a scribbled note. At the same time he made ominous stroking movements with his left hand on something in his suit pocket that made a slight bulge. He received ten money packages and dropped them into a leather bag.

Nobody else seemed to notice. The bank guard wasn't anywhere in sight. Sherdell, who had come into the bank to cash one of his small weekly paychecks, automatically whirled on his heels. In seconds after the man in the rumpled suit had gone at a quick walk, Sherdell reached the entrance. He was breathing hard.

Rumpled Suit, with a glance around him, took one look at Sherdell's grimly determined face and ran. Sherdell followed, shouting a part of the time. He never knew how long he ran, nor did he have any idea if had attracted anybody's attention.

He slowed down when Rumpled Suit paused in front of an apartment house. The look of grim determination in his eyes was even more pronounced now than when he had started out. Suddenly Sherdell became aware of thumping footsteps in back of him. Scowling, he swung about. A policeman and a group of passersby had joined the chase.

Rumpled Suit disappeared inside the building. Sherdell followed him up a dark flight of stairs, and through a door which he blocked with his shoe before it could be slammed shut. Breathing harshly, Sherdell passed through the door, locked it behind him and stumbled across the room until he stood in front of the dirt-encrusted fire-escape window. Dust hopscotched in front of his eyes.

"Give me that bag!" Sherdell said quickly, gripping the rumpled-suited man by the arm and swinging him about. "Give it to me, or you won't get a dime out of this robbery." His voice was grating and harsh.

Surprise flared briefly in the man's eyes. It was quickly replaced by a look of stark fear. Out on the second floor landing the cop had begun hammering at the door, shouting, "Open up or I'll blast off the lock!"

Sherdell said quietly, "Hand that bag over or you're finished."

Rumple Suit blinked and relinquished the bag. Sherdell opened it, his deft fingers ruffling through the packets of bills. Half of them he thrust under the large section of carpet beneath the bureau. Then he opened the window as wide as he could.

In the hallway, the cop abandoned his intention of blasting off the lock and put his shoulder to the door.

"When he comes in, we'll be fighting," Sherdell said, putting the bag on the window ledge. "Quick now, or neither of us will ever get his share of the loot."

To conceal his real intention he cocked a fist and then, drawing a deep breath, he gripped the rumple-suited man by the throat. Relentlessly, despite the other's feeble struggles, he applied steady pressure with his thumbs until the man's face grew livid and his tongue protruded.

Before Sherdell let him sag to the floor he went through his pockets and took possession of his keys, knowing he'd have to return to the room as soon as possible to pick up the money he'd hidden under the carpet.

The door finally crashed open, and the cop staggered into the room, recovering his balance with an effort. For an instant he stood staring down grimly at the slumped form on the floor.

Sherdell said coolly, "I was in the bank when he started dumping money into that bag. I followed him here. Maybe I killed him. I was trying to save the bank's money, but I might've lost some of it." He gestured at the bag, tilted to one side on the window ledge, then up to the opened window.

The cop walked over to Sherdell and suddenly hit him, flush on the jaw. "You damned lying murderer!"

"I don't know what you're talking about."

"Then hear me good," the cop snapped. "The man you killed was Benny Steele. He's a mute—can't talk."

"Mute?" Sherdell felt dizzy. "But he—he was robbing the bank. He ran away from me."

"He ran because you started to chase him," the cop said sharply. "He was running from you. Maybe you thought at first that he was a crook. But he was right in figuring that you were one."

The cop walked over to the leather bag and pulled out the note giving a list of denominations in which the mute man had wanted the money. Underneath was a bank book. No doubt a withdrawal slip in Benny Steele's name was back at the bank.

Stephen Sherdell gasped.

"He was an honest customer who was taking out a lot of his own money, that's all," the cop said. "Now, where's the dough *you* stole from him?"

A KNIFE FOR MY LOVE

Steve Page sat at the dinner table and watched his wife talking to his boss. His wife Archie, for Alexandra, rose briefly and gathered the folds of her low-cut black dress around her to the sound of soft crackles.

"What does a man see in a woman? A good figure," she pointed down to hers, "and well-shaped legs. You don't know what goes on," a long thin forefinger tapped her head, "here."

"Steve ought to know—and do something about it, if he has to." His boss, Louis Honnicutt, chuckled. "If you knew your wife suddenly fell for another man, wouldn't you kill her?"

Archie smiled, asking Steve coolly, "Could you bring yourself to do that to me?"

Steve took a long breath, then said something pleasant about the job he did for Honnicutt. He forced himself to smile.

Quickly he put his shaking hands below the table. His heart thundered.

Honnicutt, getting up to leave, cleared his throat with a chopping sound that all his employees hated.

"You're lucky, Steve, to be married to such a fine girl.

Makes me wish I had a wife, too." He leaned forward heavily and kissed Archie on the cheek. "A brotherly peck—Ha! Ha! I'm sure your husband won't mind."

After he left the smell of liquor stayed in the air while Steve and Archie washed and wiped the dishes.

"He must have a lot of money," Archie said thoughtfully. "You can sense it."

Steve shrugged. He seldom said a bad-tempered word.

"If you'd met him before you met me, things might have been different, huh?"

He glanced at Archie, but her lips were rigid. He stared in hopes of seeing the slightest ripple of amusement in her at what he'd just said.

"How much money do you suppose he's got?"

"Three hundred thousand or so."

Steve was always prompt with figures. He had a good head for them.

"It's only money, kid," he added, smiling.

"My parents married for love," she said faintly, "and when their money ran short they started to hate each other."

"Let's not go overboard about money, then."

He looked up hopefully. An irritable shrug died in her shoulders and she smiled back. But she was thoughtful. Later that night in the bedroom as she sat before the mirror and stroked her smooth black hair, she paused suddenly and turned to him.

"Steve, how much money do you make a year? Fifty-five hundred. Do any of your friends make more?"

"Not my close friends. You know that."

He meant men with whom he had spent an occasional stag evening up till three months ago, when he'd gotten married.

Steve lay back. He was in bed, but his body rested over the quilt. He wore a pair of bedroom slippers Archie had given him for his birthday.

"How many men do you know," she asked, "who make much more?"

"Maybe one or two in the office."

"You don't think much about making money? About being able to afford the things you dreamed about when you were a kid?"

"Most people grow up and get a few square meals under their belts and stop thinking about it," he said lazily. "If you don't feel that way, why'd you hook up with me?"

"Maybe I was getting tired of a lot of things. Tired and a little lonesome." She tucked away her comb for the last time that night and got to her feet.

"And now you've had a few square meals." He flushed. His hands were shaking again, so badly that he had to thrust them under the pillow and flop around on his stomach.

Archie sat down next to him. Her soft warm hands ruffled his hair so that he had to turn and hold the warmth of her in his arms.

"Don't you worry, Steve." Her breath circulated air around his left ear. "By the way, I invited Lou Honnicutt to the party tomorrow night. You don't mind, do you?"

She lay down next to him. Steve ran a hand through her soft black hair, then raised himself on his elbows....

* * * * * * *

At the party Saturday night, Steve saw an old friend looking from him, Steve, to the sleek, beautifully-turned-out Archie, then shaking his head in surprise.

Archie, in a corner, talked to Louis Honnicutt. Her wet white teeth showed in a smile. As Honnicutt talked, he drew curves in the air with palms parallel.

Steve circled them often, then moved as best he could through the living room. It was cluttered with many-colored crepe papers criss-crossing each other. Every table held a canapé tray.

Once he danced—Archie had taught him how. For the rest of the time, he sat and looked down past the surface of his deep, heavy, filled glass. When he talked to anybody, his words ran together.

Steve woke up in bed the next morning. He had crumpled the sheets and, if his sense of smell wasn't making a fool out of him, thrown up sometime in the night.

"Lou put you to bed," Archie said, after Steve finally swallowed an aspirin.

"Guess I've no business drinking." He felt his face redden. "Lou? Honnicutt?"

"I'm not going to run away with him, Steve, so don't flip." She added thoughtfully, "Even if I did, there are more good faces and bodies where mine came from."

"What you're doing now is rationalizing," he said.

"Trying to make excuses for what you've already decided to do." He blinked. "If I thought for a minute...."

He looked down to the pink bathrobe flowing evenly around her body.

A cynical look crossed Archie's smooth lovely face. "You wouldn't give a tumble to the same girl in another body."

"Do you think I'm just interested in what we do at night?"

She shrugged. "Any man, no matter who, falls in love with a girl's physical appearance and nothing else. 'Love' fades out, but money sticks to a man who's rich enough."

"You don't believe that!" Steve bounded forward, taking her by the shoulders. "This is just nonsense, isn't it?"

She smiled faintly. "If that's what you want to think."

"You're just trying to make me jealous."

"I suppose so." She pecked his cheek. "I wouldn't want to see you upset, Steve. You're a good guy."

All the same, he was growing restless. He talked to her very seldom and when he did, he sounded nasty, bitter, ungrateful. He wasn't able to apologize with words, but when he looked at her she shrugged and said nothing at all.

H spent some nights by himself, mostly going to the movies. Before meeting Archie he had seen three or four movies a week by himself.

Lingering over his second cup of breakfast coffee on a morning two months later, he watched Archie join him at the table. Her tidy black housedress (she was almost always dressed for breakfast) was just about covered by a red-edged apron. Weak pencils of sunlight slanted through the kitchen window straight at her face.

She hesitated, avoiding his eyes. Finally, she took off the apron and set it down at one side, then looked up.

"There's something I have to tell you."

Steve grew rigid. He forced himself to put the coffee cup on the napkin set in the saucer. His hand was steady.

"Go on. Don't let me stop you, Archie."

"Last night, Lou Honnicutt asked me to marry him."

He made a fist below the table. His other hand gripped a leg of it so hard that he felt splinters in his palm.

"I told Lou I'd let him know my answer over lunch."

"You've been seeing each other," he said slowly. His eyes burned.

"There's been no funny business between me and Lou," she said quickly. "I couldn't let it happen, I'd spoil my biggest attraction in his eyes."

"You're going to marry him?"

"It's the kind of break I've always dreamed about, Steve," she said simply.

Steve felt a certain relief that the decision had been made, that the tension was over. But the feeling couldn't last long.

"It's been good to know you, Steve, like the song

says. I wish...well, there's no use talking about it, if I can't ever feel secure with you. But you're such a good guy!"

Archie leaned forward earnestly, a hand outstretched for his. She smiled slightly, pausing before she spoke, probably trying to find the right words.

"There are a lot of pretty girls in the world," she said finally. "Beautiful girls, girls who make me look sick by comparison. You'll find one and settle down."

Steve muttered something, then got up from the table and walked to the window.

"You'll be more sure of yourself with women than you used to be," she added. "And as I say, Steve, there are plenty of good figures around."

"And you're sure," he said slowly, "that all I ever needed you for was to sleep with."

Steve faced the window, staring down at the people below. Then he turned and without a look back to her, left the apartment. Outside in the hall, he leaned back against a wall and held his head in his hands.

He got through the morning's work, somehow. In the afternoon, he was called into Honnicutt's private office. The boss held out the telephone receiver to him.

"Steve?" Archie said. "I wanted to tell you something else this morning, but you left too quickly."

"Go ahead."

"I was hoping that you'd meet me at the county court-house at nine-thirty tomorrow morning for a preliminary hearing on our divorce."

"So soon?"

"Lou wants it over with right away—and he knows enough people in power to let him cut a few corners." She laughed warmly. "Remember what I told you about the advantages in having plenty of money?"

He mumbled and muttered something incoherent back into the phone. His hands were sweaty.

She added pleasantly, "You'll get over it, Steve."

He put down the receiver slowly. His hands, sunk into his pockets, formed fists.

Honnicutt cleared his throat. "I hope we can forget about any personal complaints, Steve, and get along with the work. You're a valuable man around here, you know."

He was shamefacedly avoided Steve's eyes as he suggested the raise Steve had been wanting for six months.

Late that night, Steve came back to a silent apartment. He wandered through it a little dazed, mechanically straightening a pillow or wiping a speck of dust away. He gazed for half an hour at the bedroom slippers Archie had given him.

Slowly, he walked to the bedroom closet. He pulled down a battered leather suitcase. Inside it were a few odds and ends. In a sheath was a thick, stubby knife. Steve ran a finger over the sides and the tip. He repacked the suitcase except for the knife, and got into bed.

He stood in front of the narrow side-entrance of the large gray stone courthouse building on the next morning. Raw as the weather was, he hesitated before putting his cold hands in his pockets. When he did, two fingers touched the knife-edge inside.

In the last twenty minutes, he had walked through the building, looking carefully and asking sharp questions before finally making up his mind.

More than six dozen people had come into the building while he waited outside; the frightened litigants and smooth-looking lawyers, the contented clerks and even a bowler-hatted judge. Steve was sure he had picked them all out correctly.

He was shrugging his coat collar tight against his neck to protect it from the raw weather when he heard the familiar rhythm of Archie's footsteps. He looked up quickly.

The outfit she wore, the way she looked, even the tilt of her head, all had associations for him. She smiled politely, even cordially, at him.

Steve was calm. "I have to go up to see an old friend of mine first. He's in Room Three-Nine-Seven."

"I'll meet you in Room Six-One, Judge Passy's chambers."

"Let's go up and see my friend first. Won't take more than five minutes."

Archie shrugged; probably Lou had advised her to humor him.

Room Three-Nine-Seven was old and dirty. Wherever Steve looked, from the scratched file cabinets to an old-style, broad-beamed safe in one corner, was an unmarked snowbank of dust.

Within a few hours, pictures of this room would appear in newspapers, and dozens of strangers would be re-enacting with gestures what he was about to do.

Calmly, almost patiently, he locked the door. "I'm sorry, Archie."

His voice was heavy. When he turned, he looked intently at her white face.

"Steve, I suppose this is your idea of a dramatic, last-minute appeal, but I've made up my mind to go through with it. I wish I didn't feel the way I do, but there it is. So if you'll open the door...."

Steve took the long, tapering knife out of a pocket.

"Put that away," she said irritably. "What do you think you're doing?"

Steve raised the knife. Advancing on her, he circled a horse-tail of her hair around one hand. Her knees were suddenly hard against his.

At every knife-thrust against her face, his sobs were mingled with the shrieks out of Archie's throat.

He didn't try to cover her mouth; the room was soundproof.

When he stepped back, Archie fell forward to the floor. Her feet kicked, her hands pounded. Steve talked to the back of her head to make himself heard.

"I'm sorry, baby, I had to do it."

The feet and hands went still. Finally, her sobs stopped, too.

"You should have killed me, instead."

"Why? Because your wealthy boyfriend Louis Honnicutt won't look at you any more. Is that it?"

"Nobody will. Nobody could."

"I can."

He was aware of her turning slowly. She covered her blood-streaked face with her hands, but the tear-shot eyes were suddenly sharp.

He said carefully, "I love you pretty—and I love you ugly. I'll want to be with you when I'm a hundred."

"You could go to jail for this."

"I'll take my chances." He rose slowly. "I'll call for first aid."

As he hesitated, her hand reached out for his. Steve took it, smiled, then bent over and gently kissed his wife's scarred face.

KILLER IN THE BLEACHERS

Detective Steve Ames beamed down at his young son sitting next to him. "To kids a big moment in baseball is like a lighted Christmas tree," he said, turning to his partner, Robert Fuller. "That's why we're here. Stevie Junior likes the real stuff better than television."

He was trying to arrange himself so that his toes wouldn't always be squeezed up against the back of the seat in front of him here in the bleachers. Suddenly he became rigid, forgetting the game almost completely. He looked down at the crowded rows of seats which sloped to the green of the outfield. He stared for almost a full minute, then glanced at his partner.

"Bob, look down to the second row. Isn't that Rock Wilson?"

Ames had to nudge Bob Fuller twice before his handsome partner took notice of the man six rows beneath him—a serious-looking young man.

"The whole force has been after him since he disappeared a year ago," Ames whispered. "He always carries a gun and boasts that if he's caught a cop will get it, too."

"The crowd's too big for us to do anything now," Bob Fuller said. He turned to his partner's other side. "Keep your eyes on the batter, Junior," he said. "That's Fred Jensen."

Steve Ames nodded his small blond head with all the patience he'd learned in eight years of living, and craned his neck to see what was happening on the field.

'There's the three-two pitch—and a walk," Fuller explained to his partner's child. "A sacrifice will get Jensen to second, but the pitcher is the man to watch now. He's great!"

"Forget the game for a minute, can't you?" Ames snapped. "Didn't you and that hood have a tank room session a few years ago? He's sure to remember that grilling if he sees you now, and he's wanted for *murder*. That pitcher out there isn't worrying about staying one jump ahead of the electric chair."

"I'll wait out of sight until we can pick him up, if I can't think of any other way to get him," Bob Fuller said, standing. "Should I take Junior with me?"

"No," Ames said firmly. "You must be out of your mind. If he should see you and Stevie in the last row together—"

Fuller walked out of the aisle, but the inconvenience to others at an unexpectedly tense moment in the game resulted in noises that rippled downwards. Abruptly the killer turned. His coal-black eyes rested briefly on Fuller, then swung back to the empty seat next to the taut-faced detective and the small boy at his side. Ames sat perfectly still, and tormented by the fact that he wasn't carrying a gun.

Stevie Ames, gazing to his right, suddenly said in a conversational tone, "Uncle Bob must like baseball an awful lot."

"He sure does," Ames said through his teeth. "But don't get soda pop on your pants."

There was noise from the crowd again and the killer, avoiding Bob Fuller's previous mistake, got up inconspicuously and trained his gaze on Ames sitting there with his son.

Ames glanced around for just a second, hoping to catch sight of Bob Fuller. But his partner wasn't in the aisle at all. How stupid could you get? If Fuller had gone to make a call for reinforcements it would be far too late by the time they arrived. Rock Wilson was certainly going to make his move first.

Ames wiped his red face with a handkerchief and made an attempt to dry part of his shirt by stretching its back away from his body.

Wilson started walking up the concrete stairs. Almost before Ames realized it, Wilson was stepping past a row of drawn-up legs, and making his way to the detective's side.

"The kid comes with me," he said to Ames. His voice was soft, almost friendly. But Ames could hear it distinctly above the restless chattering of fans and the tired chants of the venders. "If the kid's with me, I'm safe."

"Now wait a minute," Ames protested, his voice hoarse with strain. "I don't know you. You've made a mistake—"

"Don't tell me you're not a cop! I've been watching you. I can tell. And don't try to make me think your buddy, who I know personally, isn't phoning, right now, for more cops." Then to Stevie. "Come on, kid, you're taking a walk."

Ames reached out with his right hand to keep his now frightened little boy close to him.

"I can give it to him right here or send him back if he behaves," the killer said quickly. "Which do you— *uhhh!*"

Rock Wilson whirled around, wide-eyed, clapped his hand to his brow and swayed like a drunken man for an instant. Then his knees gave way and he collapsed across two hastily emptied seats in a downward plunge that sent his drawn gun spinning and Ames grabbed it instantly.

Amidst a flurry of startled spectators in the immediate vicinity one man held up a grimy baseball. "Where did this come from?" he asked, puzzled.

Steve Ames spun around to the nearest aisle. Bob Fuller was standing not too far away next to the uniformed player with a glove in one hand. Ames recognized him as one of the great pitchers in baseball. He realized that the ballplayer had used perfect control in aiming a baseball directly at the killer.

Fuller came over to them while Rock Wilson was being taken away on a stretcher, and smiled at Stevie Junior.

"Wasn't that a great pitch, Stevie?" he said, chuckling.

Steve Ames swore under his breath. Fuller was a nice guy and all, but he never took anything seriously.

LETTERS FROM BARBARA

Barbara Adams looked a lot older than sixteen, what with her full figure and sad, hollow-eyed face. She was walking despondently along Carmody Street, but there was a hard glitter in her eyes with every step she took.

At the corner she was halted by an awkward-looking boy with a thrust-out underlip and unruly hair.

"So you're back, huh, Barbara?" the boy asked. "Did you tell the cops what you said you would?"

"I sure did," Barbara said, not being able to keep the self-satisfaction out of her voice. "It'll be a long time before Duke James is out of prison once the cops come for him. He's going to find out how dull things can get."

"You told the cops everything?"

"I told 'em the truth. I told 'em that I wouldn't ever have taken heroin if not for Duke James. If he hadn't conned me into it by telling me how great it was. Then I said I'd never have had to hit the streets if I hadn't needed money to buy the H with. I said and I meant that it's Duke's fault."

The boy called Frog looked even more uncomfortable than usual. "Maybe you shouldn't 'a done that,

Barbara. Duke, he gets kind of vengeful."

"Duke was always saying he had big plans for me," Barbara smiled. "Well, now, I'm the one who's got a plan for him. And quite a plan it is, Frog."

She was going to say something more when she felt a hard hand against hers. A grip was caught before she could even call out, and she turned around to face the handsome youngster with curly black hair and strong-looking teeth that gleamed with wolfish anger.

"I hear that the cops are looking for me and that it's your fault," Duke James said crisply. "Right?"

"That's right," Barbara said. "You'll be going to a place that's very dull, and where you can't have any good times at all. Isn't that too ba—?"

One of Duke James's hands came up like a whip cracking against Barbara's gaunt face. He hit her again and again in spite of Frog's presence and in spite of the people who turned to look. Nobody stopped him.

When he was finished with her, he took a step back and scowled at Frog.

"You're smarter than I thought, fella, not mixing up in this. A lot smarter."

He turned and walked away. Barbara, swaying where she stood, scowled after him but didn't say a word that Duke James could've made out. "I've got big plans for you, Duke," she said, as he moved out of hearing distance. "*Very* big plans." She glanced to one side. "Want to see how I'll get even with the fellow who destroyed me?"

Frog didn't especially want to see anything, but he'd

have liked to get Barbara away from this block. You never knew if Duke might not take it into his head to come back and give the girl more punishment.

"Yeh," he said quickly. "Sure, Barbara."

"Okay, come along."

She led the way to a nearby housing project and into the hall. Avoiding the elevator they walked six flights, Barbara in the lead. Every so often she would glance back to make sure that Frog was following her.

In a wide apartment, she walked into a small room with a folding bed against one wall. She reached into a bureau drawer and took out a bottle, then pulled out three sheets of stiff white paper from a cardboard box. In the bathroom she drew out a wide glass and filled it with sink water.

"Here goes," she muttered.

From the bottle Barbara took two white capsules and emptied them into the wide glass. Then she threw in a sheet of paper. She pulled out the paper after several minutes had passed. She emptied the glass, filled it again, and repeated the process with a fresh sheet of paper. She did it a third time, too.

With the glass emptied, Barbara took the three curly sheets of paper and placed them on a nearby ironing board, then plugged in the iron sitting atop it. She waited a few minutes, then checked the iron's warmth with the tip of a moistened finger. Satisfied, she proceeded to carefully iron both sides of each sheet of paper. When she was finished, the papers looked as they had originally, just a little stiffer, and very white, probably from the powder grains which had soaked into the papery fibers.

She said quickly, "Sit down at the kitchen table."

Frog, who hadn't uttered a word during all this, said, "Sure," and proceeded to follow her instructions. He stared at the sight of the first sheet of paper pushed in front of him along with a ball-point pen.

"Okay, Frog, now write what I say: 'Dear Duke, Everything here is all right. Dad is fine. Hope you are well. Love, Mother'."

She dictated two other similar letters and then passed across three envelopes, on which Frog wrote Duke's real name, Herman James, and an address that she gave him. Barbara must have looked up the location of the detention place where male prisoners were held.

"I'll send out the first letter in a few days," Barbara chortled. "By the time Duke gets it he'll be bored to insanity, and he'll do anything for the thrill of it, or an extra ounce of pleasure. He'll know the handwriting is phony, and he'll figure out that he's supposed to tear off a strip of paper at a time and chew it to get a buzz."

"And the other two letters, too." A tide of nausea was rising in Frog. "He won't have enough willpower to resist it, though he'll know it'll destroy him in time. You'll have made him an addict because he made you one."

"And the slickest part of it," Barbara smiled, "is that he'll be so depressed that he'll be sure I'm doing him a favor."

THE ONE AND ONLY

Ford Kelvey was let out of prison a little less than five years after he was sent in. Three hours after hopping the train at Ossining, he was back in New York City where he belonged.

The West Village had changed, turning dull and middle-class. A buddy from the old days did show up at a bar Kelvey had known when somebody else ran it. Right away, of course, he asked about Abe Singer. Honest Abie, as the little Jew was known, had bought into a good business. Kelvey knew bitterly where the money had come from. Not one of the guys who used to buddy up with him saw Abie these days. In fact, somebody else had let Kelvey's informant know about Abe having moved away and got married.

Kelvey found Abe's name in the phone book, with a small b after it for business location. A girl at the other end told him sunnily that Mr. Singer would be back from a working trip on Friday and could see him in the morning.

"He'd better see me," Kelvey said thinly. "You make sure an' tell him that."

"What was the message again? The girl asked,

maybe on account of not being used to somebody who talked so plainly.

Ford Kelvey was too angry to repeat it. It was strange how he never had any dealings with Abie Singer that didn't involve him or Singer not getting things straight.

It wasn't that long ago that Kelvey had asked Abe for a favor to drive a borrowed car half a dozen blocks and wait for him a few minutes. Singer hadn't figured that a bank robbery was on his acquaintance's schedule. He certainly couldn't have expected to hear shots and see a wounded Kelvey limping out to the car, let alone the chase that had followed.

Even as Kelvey settled back in the car, he remembered, his mind was working fast. "Take this bag and scoot," he snapped. "You'll give me what's in there some other time."

"Every penny," Abe Singer had promised fervently. "One way or another you'll get every penny back."

Although Kelvey was in pain and could guess what his immediate future was going to be like, he didn't hesitate to trust Abe Singer. The little Jew's uprightness was a watchword among those gamblers with whom he hung out and whose lifestyle had fascinated him.

Until now, it seemed." This is the last time I ever let myself get mixed up with somebody like you," Singer said, reaching for the black bag because it wasn't any part of his nature to let somebody down. "From now on, I only make friends with Yeshiva men and rabbis, so help me! Word of honor."

"Never mind the yapping!"

"But you'll get this money somehow."

A police car could be heard racing up the avenue.

Honest Abie, as people called him, the briefcase under one arm, rushed to the end of the alley. Only once did he look back, then he walked out like a businessman on the way to some big meeting. Most likely he was too scared to do any more of the rushing his insides were crying out for him to do. Well, the guy had two legs in decent condition and he could move 'em!

Kelvey forced himself to get behind the driver's seat. He was trying to stanch the blood from his left calf when the police car swerved into the mouth of the alley.

One previous arrest some fifteen years back was enough to make Kelvey remember what was likely to happen next. A sergeant named Paxton put him over the jumps after his wound had been treated. Over and over Kelvey repeated that he didn't know zitz about any bank money and that he wanted a lawyer.

He found himself being represented by a beefy guy named Callahan, who notified him quietly that a friend was paying the fee in secret to make sure Kelvey got the best possible representation. Kelvey knew perfectly well who that friend was. With anybody but Honest Abie he'd have figured that the payout was insurance to keep an arrested bank robber from telling who else had been in the car with him. Abie, though, had a head that worked along lines Kelvey could never anticipate.

Even a former friend had to be helped out, by Abie if there wasn't anybody else to raise a hand.

It wasn't hard to guess where Abie had gotten the money. Kelvey could've done without that. Better to have the stuff waiting for him on the outside. Abie was different, that was all.

The trial was short, and didn't get much publicity because a city scandal was taking up a lot of space in the New York papers. Callahan did an okay job, but was busting his head against a wall and Kelvey knew it. The jury came in with its verdict after only five minutes, and Kelvey thought he was lucky to draw easy numbers like seven to ten, with two down for good behavior.

He kept to himself for those first grim months at Ossining, not making friends or even getting mixed up in the secret gambling games. Honest Abie sent money once a month through a mutual friend. It came in useful to buy some things, but he'd rather have had the loot when he was sprung. He tried to get that message through, but Abie must have thought the other guy was lying for some reason. The dough kept coming. Again Kelvey wasn't seeing eye to eye with the Jew.

But Kelvey couldn't keep to himself for the next few years. Listening to prisoners—to *other* prisoners— meant hearing that they considered everybody outside as having done them dirt. He supposed he was being influenced, after a while. Spending the money from Abe on a secret high-stake game was the tipoff that he had changed.

In hardly any time he was starting to think about himself as another victim, somebody who had been put upon. Abie Singer must be living off the fat of the land with money Kelvey had given him and was suffering for. Every once in a while he'd break his heart to send a few bucks in, that Jew who was making a dandy profit while Ford Kelvey did time, his waist getting thicker, his eyes more hollow, his face white and then gray. It didn't need much more talk from the others for him to decide that when he got replanted out of this place, the damned Jew would give him every remaining nickel of that stolen money plus interest! One way or another, as Honest Abie himself had said, the guy was going to pay for that freedom—through his Jewish nose if necessary.

Ford Kelvey would make sure about that.

Abe Singer, like Kelvey himself, had got thicker in the waist and his features were fuller. He was dressed in fine threads, though, a two-piece "gun-check" suit with matching vest, a cotton shirt and silk club tie.

"You can see I worked hard." He waved at the busy outer office. "And I've been lucky, with the help of the *Rabbaynu shol oylom.*"

"I don't understand that chicken talk." Kelvey looked stonily at the window with Abe's name in gold flake, and the words Real Estate Broker. "You've had five good years with my money."

Singer's face was flushing. "I bought into this business with it, yes, and made enough to buy out my partner. As for the amount of my stake, I returned it anonymously and with interest to the bank as soon as possible. What I gave you was extra and out of my own pocket."

"I told you to give me back the dough later on," Kelvey snapped. "Anything else you did cuts no ice with me."

He couldn't help being sore. Never had he heard of anybody giving back money to the bank it had been stolen from! Thanks to that little Jew, his prison term had been for nothing—if he accepted what he was being told. For enough money, Honest Abie could probably lie his head off, too. Just like everybody else.

"And you think I owe you everything in that brief-case except the money I sent you?" Singer asked.

"I know it, Abe, and I'm here to get just that."

Singer considered. "I could probably quote you from the Torah until you-know-what freezes over, but you'd never change your mind."

"Not about the green stuff I wouldn't!"

"I've already paid out much more than you gave me to hold for you, and it's beyond me that you have any real right to consider yourself the owner. All the same, that money was very useful to me. Without it, I wouldn't be in this business or married or have one child and another on the way, God willing."

"Okay, so you owe me."

"Not only is money very tight these days, but this whole thing is a problem in ethics, in common decency. I have to ask advice what to do."

"Advice from who?"

"From my rabbi, from, probably, other wise and oly men. From the local *amorayeem*, the jurists, so to speak."

"You'd tell some strangers what happened?"

"I wouldn't mention your name, should that prospect upset you."

"Well, if you want to hand yourself over on a plate, that's up to you."

"These men are my friends and advisers," Singer whispered.

"Just the same, Abie, I can't wait longer for the rest of that money."

"Not even one extra day? Give me twenty-four hours to—no, make it on Sunday morning. Tomorrow is the *shabb*—it would take too long to explain. Leave your phone number and I'll be in touch on Sunday morning."

"You'd better be in touch," Kelvey said carefully, making himself as clear as possible. "And you'd better pay up what's coming to me. I don't want to make threats, but if I do I'll carry out every one of 'em should you force me into that."

"I'll do what's right."

"You've got two days, Jew-boy, and don't you forget it!"

He walked out of there, favoring his left leg, and went back to his hotel. It was the same place on Eighteenth Street where he had lived more than a dozen years ago, and privacy was certain. The prices had gone up out of all knowledge or sense in the meantime, but a similar complaint held good for just everything in the city to which he had returned.

Twenty minutes after he woke up on Sunday morning, Kelvey's phone rang. Abe Singer was on the other end.

"Be in my office tomorrow morning at eleven," Singer said.

"You don't have to tell me that, Abie. One way or the other I'll be there."

Singer was dressed more quietly this time, and his cheeks looked a little sunken. Taking the visitor's chair confidently, Kelvey didn't feel a bit surprised that the Jew had chosen to pay up instead of facing violence.

"I have been advised to pay you enough so that the use of the money will have cost me double in penalties," Singer said quietly.

"How much is that?"

A briefcase was passed across to him. Inside Kelvey found eight thousand dollars in used and unmarked small bills. Kelvey had hoped for more, but after Singer's previous expenses this amount seemed just about on the nose.

"I've also been advised to tell you that this is all you're getting," Singer added. "The gravy train stops right here."

"We can worry about that some other time, Abie."

He zipped the case shut. In this cheerful mood he didn't give a solitary damn about what might happen next year. He wouldn't be bothered to understand how intensely Abie was talking and that as a result probably every word was serious. The loot he had earned and suffered for, that loot or what was left of it, was now in his hands.

Spending money in the Big Apple had never been much of a problem for Kelvey. With a stake like his, it was only a matter of some short time before he had taken up with an expensive good-looker who kept an office humming by day and kept Kelvey humming at night. He didn't deny himself any goods he wanted. Hadn't he put in time upstate for this? Well, he was going to get the best of everything while even a penny of his stake lasted.

By December he was on the phone to Abe Singer again. This time he didn't get through till he'd just about promised to tear the receptionist apart otherwise.

"I need a loan," he said without any introduction when Singer came on.

"A loan that'll never get paid back, huuh?" Singer said, and added flatly, "Sorry, but I'm not a finance company."

"Then I'm going to sing real pretty to the cops, Abie. Don't tell me you want your wife and kid to see their old man in jail."

"*You'd* be there for sure," the Jew said spiritedly. "Besides, I'm not guilty of anything at all in this matter."

"I'll be in to see you for that next eight thousand, Jew-boy, and you'd better have it."

"If you come up here again," Abe Singer began, and Kelvey broke the connection with a laugh just after the Jew solemnly promised to have a private eye on duty at his office.

Kelvey didn't take the threat seriously. No private op would risk his life to do any job, and Kelvey was going to make sure a possible death threat was plain and might be put into action against client and peeper.

It meant buying a gun and bullets. The only dealers he knew from the old days were in the can themselves or had gone to Florida or Arizona for the winter warmth. One of his few remaining old-time friends put Kelvey through to a young guy of not more than twenty and known as Geezer, for some reason. Maybe the word for an old man meant something different these days. A hell of a lot of other things had changed!

Once it was clear to Geezer that Ford Kelvey didn't want to buy a broad a bag or a deck, negotiations went ahead smoothly.

"Give me two hours," Geezer said. They were at a small table in the bar called Freddy's. "Meet you right here."

Geezer was five minutes better than his word, coming back with a blue steel .32 S&W long and a dozen bullets.

"This doesn't look like it could make much of a hole," Kelvey grumbled in vague hopes of driving the price down.

"Are you puttin' me on, man? This baby would make a hole a truck could drive through."

Kelvey nodded as if it made for a decisive answer. The price would leave him with no more than a hundred dollars and the urgent need for money. Enough to make

Abe Singer's life miserable, for sure.

By the time he got back to his hotel with the merchandise, night had fallen. He'd have gone directly to the Jew's home and scared the life out of the man's family, but wanted to save that as a further threat in case of need. Not that he expected the least difficulty. A Jew was likely to know what self-interest called for. Singer could swear angrily to hire all the private dicks in the world and actually do it, but when push came to shove he'd want to play it safe.

Kelvey spent a quiet night in front of the television set watching a hockey game on some cable channel. Sleep was never a problem for him and he got up refreshed in the morning. He put on the dark suit they'd handed him at Ossining, and added a checkered cap he had bought since coming out. Satisfied that the combination made him look dangerous to Singer and any private detective who might come around, Kelvey added a coat and set out at last.

A breakfast stop took only fifteen minutes. By nine-thirty he got busy walking. The time it took him was enough for Singer definitely to be at his desk. This being Friday, he'd want to quit early for the Jewish Sabbath, so he'd probably come iin early as well.

Another decision Kelvey had made was to stand for no nonsense whatever. Let him bull his way through, cutting some private Richard down to size, and Singer wouldn't hesitate now or the next time Kelvey made a request for money. Or the time after that and so on.

By half-past ten he was in the Thirties, the neighborhood of Singer's office building. He found the right one easily.

Singer's outer office was crowded, two staff women back of a railing and visitors on chairs at this side. A perky young secretary smiled up at him.

"I have an appointment with Singer."

"And your name, please?"

He gave it.

The girl put through a brief call. Her face was more composed when she looked back. "I'm afraid you'll have to wait your turn, sir."

"The hell I will!" He walked to the quarter-sized swinging door which would let him into the other part of the room and to Singer's office door down at the far end.

One of the visitors called, "Hey, mister, we've all got to wait."

Kelvey whirled around. Two women were sitting with snarly brats, and there was a bearded man in his forties. This man wore a skullcap and a suit darker than Kelvey's. Probably one of those synagogue buddies of Abe Singer's, and hoping to get a good deal on account of the connection.

"Did you say something?"

"No, I did not," the man replied in a faintly European-accented English. His voice was deeper than that of the man who had just spoken. "My name is Joseph "Einhorn, and—"

Kelvey had already looked away to the last chair in the office. It was taken by a young man in his late twenties, a young man whose cobalt blue eyes were meeting his.

"You wanted something, bo?"

"Just to remind you that everybody has to wait for Mr. Singer."

"I don't. If you want to make something out of that, just say the word."

He sensed he must be facing the private eye that Singer had told him would be on the job.

The man said, "I'm not willing to fight about it, if that's what you mean."

"Then there's something else." He drew out his gun. The women gasped. Mr. Joseph Einhorn's lips were pulled down disapprovingly, but that was all, as Kelvey saw from the corner of an eye. As for the private peeper, he winced as if this was his first time in front of a revolver.

"Come on, you, march in front of me."

"But I—"

"You won't get hurt if you do like I say. Get up and march in front of me to Singer's office."

He had decided on hustling the p.i. in there so that the Jew could see for himself the hired man hadn't been of the least use.

The young private peeper stood slowly, hands raised without his having to be told. Kelvey took several steps back, allowing the young man to walk in front of him and keep a safe distance.

"Okay, now get a move on."

The secretary was watching, awe-struck. One of

the children suddenly let out a squall of fear. Kelvey gestured him forward.

Singer's office door opened on a woman and child who walked at the owner's side. Singer suddenly looked out and over the office. His eyes came to the young man, then moved to Kelvey back of him.

Maliciously, Ford Kelvey raised his gun. "How'd you like a dose of this, Abie?"

He'd been intending to fright the Jew and nothing more, but didn't get any further. Back of him, the flat of a hand suddenly cracked at his neck, forcing him to gasp and turn. The gun was useless. A fist crashed against his right cheek, twisting his neck again and knocking out at least one tooth while sending him down to the floor.

A foot was on his gun hand, remaining there and exerting hellish pressure till he let go of the weapon. Then he was raised by the lapel. The attacker was bringing up a fist and one sure haymaker to the jaw. In the split second before it landed, Kelvey managed to get one anguished look at the man's face. He damn well knew that he must have misunderstood Honest Abie once more, and this had been the most important time of all. Just the same his eye opened wide in disbelief....

"You couldn't 'a done that better if you'd been one of those private detectives on television," the sergeant said to the bearded Jew. He had been assigned to take care of this emergency call.

Joseph Einhorn smiled. "I am not a private detective

by any means, sergeant. In Europe I was nothing more than a *boolvon*, a bully. This job I took on because Mr. Singer is an important person at the syngagoue and was in the right when he dealt with this man. What's more, Mr. Singer asked for help."

Kelvey, hands cuffed back of him and a uniformed policeman watchfully at his side, was dazed and furious. He certainly knew he'd been shafted. Singer had sworn to have a p.i. on the premises—it was hard to remember exactly what term the guy had used, but that'd been his point beyond the least doubt—and instead this big Jewish ox had been the one to look out for. How in hell could Ford Kelvey have known it beforehand?

"Well," the sergeant said to Mr. Einhorn, noticing the skullcap at last. "You did a great job, Rabbi."

"I'm not a rabbi, either," Einhorn smiled. "I am a functionary at my synagogue, yes, but I have only the job of making sure there's no disorder during services and that all ceremonies proceed smoothly."

"Sort of a policeman yourself, in a way, without a badge." The sergeant frowned in thought. "What you mean is that you're like a sexton."

"Perfectly correct, sergeant. In Hebrew and Yiddish I am called a *shamus*...what's the matter with him?"

"Quit kicking around like that, you, or I'll settle you down good," the sergeant warned. "Come on, you're going back to jail till you can be sent upstate again for violation of parole and a few other goodies I'll be glad to think of. You've got a long trip ahead."

YOU DON'T
NEED AN ENEMY

This story I'm going to tell you is the absolute truth, not fact-*based*, as they say on television before showing you a pack of lies. True as it is, though, nobody believes a word I say about this trouble.

It all started after a day's work, when I was driving out to my main squeeze's apartment in Philadelphia.

She must have already been in the throes of cooking what she insisted would taste like tortillas as done by a French chef. After that the program called for me to do some main-squeezing. We weren't going to leave her place, making the cost to me just about zilch. Horny but happy, I drove with extra care.

Some damn fool in foreign-looking clothes was shuffling along the gutter on this chill-drenched October night. Traffic lights were solidly arranged against him as far as the eye could see. He moved gracefully, undaunted, dodging one car after another. Drivers called him everything on earth, of course.

"Did you pop your cork?" I snarled in my best detective manner, slowing at his side. "Get in here now, before I damn well chase you to the precinct house."

"Thank you very much," he said in some accent I didn't recognize; that first word sounded more like *thonk.*

I pushed open the door and practically had to draw him into my Accord, then drive over to the Friends' Meeting House before slamming his door shut and pointing to his seat belt. Seen closer, he didn't look any taller than fifty thumbs laid end to end, a slim character adorned with thick glasses and on the far side of his thirties.

"This is truly fine of you." The primer-style words with a slightly skewed meaning were spoken flatly; he wasn't sure where the accents fell. "All have been good to me."

"What they've been is saintly," I snapped, seeing a chance to pick up a reward for probably saving his life. "I've really got a good mind to put you under arrest for being a—a hazard to traffic."

He didn't look rattled. He actually smiled. "First I have to show you that I am under an oblige to you. Permit me to buy you a drink. I believe that it is your custom for paying a social debt. I am a stranger to this area."

I could have told *him* that.

A drink was a safer reward, I suppose, than taking what somebody might eventually call a bribe. I took him to my favorite Commerce Street bar, a paradise without jukebox and only for dedicated drinkers. Its name, Twelve Steps to the Bar, had rattled the cages of politically correct types all over Philly, and won the owner a mint in free publicity.

My new friend insisted he never drank, but he let me steer him to straight crème de menthe, a double that must have broken down his reserves. He told me his name was Teck, but didn't say from what foreign country he came. He did allow, though, that he was sorry he hadn't seen any joyous dancing under the wintry skies. (I ask you, could a hard-working police detective like make up a complaint like that? The right answer is no.)

Since R2D2 was willing to tackle the bar bill, I let myself take a third boilermaker. He smiled to see that I was enjoying this liquid payoff.

All I can remember after that is getting up with the intention of calling my girlfriend and letting her know I might be a couple of minutes late. And (surprise!) falling flat on the floor.

Which proved, I remember thinking on the next headache-filled day, that certain people shouldn't be let to reward you. Stop them with a summons or a subpoena, I say, if you have to. Haven't I got a good reason for feeling like that?

I wobbled downtown very early in the morning, not trusting myself to drive. I was working at my precinct on Spruce Street when Inga, my main squeeze, called to complain about my not having been with her last night. She finally accepted my excuse, but not without saying, "Damn you, Björn Engstrom!" a few times.

After which I went back to work, questioning a nude old man with a guitar who was sure he was Elvis comb back to life. One more time my phone did its job. The tenor voice on the other end had become jarringly familiar last night, but I still couldn't tell which foreign country he had been raised in.

"A small dark book fell out of your pocket when I was bringing you to the carriage that would take you home. I only observed it after the pilot of the vehicle fled and I will happily bring it over."

"Just put it inside an envelope, Teck, along with the ten dollar cab fare and tip that you owe me on account of you got me looped, and address it here and mail it."

"You sound unpleased with me."

"You got me in trouble with my girlfriend."

"I am guilty," Teck admitted. "I must make this right."

This ten dollars—I'd only spent four, but didn't say so—would help do that. "Just keep out of my way from now on and I'll be satisfied."

I hung up just as Elvis started to sing *Hound Dog*, making it a perfect morning.

Something else I can tell, what the people who write screenplays call a flash-forward: three full months drifted by before money and address book sailed home. Teck had sent it by Express Mail with a quick delivery absolutely guaranteed, but he had put two wrong numbers on the address. Is anybody shocked to know about that? I earned the extra money he put into the pot, if you know what I mean.

I took Inga out that night, paying with the money I had raised from selling Elvis's guitar that he was too spaced-out to miss, I'm sure. The two of us were at rest in her apartment later on when she eased herself out of bed for a slug of o.j.

"It'd be nice to go on working forever," she said in a wistful tone. "If I had a different boss it'd be perfect."

I certainly approved of her ambition and the likely return it would bring. Glancing down at the bed she had warmed so happily, I found myself asking, "Why don't we get married and hang out together all the time?"

Swedie, as I sometimes called Inga, ferried her o.j. back to bed and we talked. Finally agreeing on the objective in mind, we circled warily around the first details.

"You have to invite your friend, Teck, which sounds like an adaptation of his name so that a yahoo could say it, to the announcement party," Inga said after a thoughtful pause. "He really sort of put the whole idea of marriage into your head, being alone with no one to help him. We owe him."

"He's generous enough and pays up his obligations," I said, surprised to think I owed him anything. "Okay, if you want."

Teck had told me where he was staying, and called my office the next day. "I will be leaving this country after midnight and hope you will forgive my—ah—regressions."

I forgave his latest assault on my mother tongue, too, while I was at it. Again in spite of my better judgment, I passed on the euphoric invitation to the night's party. Of course I didn't forget to tell him that the happy couple was expecting a gift from him. He didn't seem to mind, taking it in stride.

Two dozen or so of our friends, mine and Inga's, breezed into her place to wish us well. Inga's mother had put up the money for refreshments, which was comforting. An understanding wife-to-be with an understanding mother is simply an extra blessing, if you ask me.

Teck, having adorned himself with a fresh clumsy outfit and newly polished thick glasses, came in early, congratulated us, and checked out the buffet, where he turned down everything except celery sticks and carrots. I was sniffing around him dubiously until he brought out his check.

Only then did I introduce him to Inga, just as a friend of hers came over to ask with concern if she, took was having trouble with their boss.

"He tried to grab me this afternoon," Inga said grimly. "Don't know what I'll do about him, and I hate to quit because the money is so good."

I'm pretty sure that Inga saw my nod of approval at her financial wisdom, but I didn't say a word in front of her co-worker and friend.

"If I complain to a department head," she added, looking at me out of the corner of an eye, "I might be downsized out of the firm double-quick."

"Tell your boss that I'm a heavyweight boxer." I grew more serious. "The best way is for me to come over to your office tomorrow and straighten him out."

My little buddy, Teck, had been listening intently. "I

will happily attend this matter for you, Björn, before going home. I owe you a great favor after what you did for me."

"Huh?" I didn't get his drift at all.

"I have to accomplish one favor for you. I will not be attending your wedding and intend to give you an advance gift for that happy time."

(You don't believe a word of it? I didn't believe it either, but that's exactly what he said. I know he had a strong sense of obligation, but the idea of a five-foot-and-change guy putting the fear of God into a normally built man, which I assumed the boss was, made no sense at all. Even if Teck drew a gun, it would mean nothing and only get Inga hip-deep in trouble.)

More girls had drifted in for the party while we talked. It always used to be a principle of mine that engagement parties are a great place to meet single girls and take them back to their place for a night, so I wanted to give my mature advice to Teck, although he probably wasn't sharp enough to do much with it. I owed him something in turn, if only good advice, for the generosity he had just shown me and Inga.

I looked around to tell him what was in my mind, but he had left the room.

"Your friend went out just before," one of the girls said to me. "He complained that we don't dance, of all things, and he hurried away."

"I don't like this," I said to Inga, drawing her aside as she was starting to tell another friend why she had finally decided to make an honest man of me.

"Somebody might've given Teck your boss's name and if he lives in Philly—"

"He does."

"—Teck could've looked him up in the phone book and decided to do me this favor after all."

One of Inga's co-workers, bombed out of her teeny tree from jealously at Inga's fabulous luck in cornering me, finally admitted she'd talked to Teck without any idea what harm she might be doing. She had given the name and home address that Teck wanted.

"I'd better get out and see your boss now," I told Inga while putting on a coat I'd been given by a retailer. "I'll spike Casanova and keep Teck in one piece if he's there."

"I hope you know what you're doing, dear."

I was pretty sure I did know. If Teck had got himself in trouble, he'd make me a cash or money order gift later on for getting him out of it. Saving him twice would make him more receptive to pointed hints. Yes, I knew what I was up to.

"A detective's work," I told Inga virtuously, "involves following up on strong hunches."

Floyd Zacuto lived in a multi-million dollar co-op on Brandywine, a toad hop from the Spring Gardens Institute. I had to show my department card to the doorman, the concierge and the lissome elevator girl before being wafted up to the thirtieth floor. A young woman answered after six rings, slender, light-haired and expensively dressed. The nearby TV was turned to a football game, and she was rubbing sleep out of violet eyes.

"I think that Floyd is in his home office," she volunteered after I had asked for the lizard by his first name. She pointed down a long hallway to a dark king-sized door at the end. I expected to hear noise enough for a circus parade, with Zacuto snarly and Teck doing his best to sound *macho*.

Wrong. Not a creature was stirring.

My knocking on the door changed nothing. I opened Zacuto's home office door on a lima-bean shaped desk and two olive-colored trays, one with paper, and a p.c. allied to a laser printer, twin filing cabinets, an office chair, a wastebasket with bikini-clad girls shown in design paper wrapped snuggly around its sides, two Indian throw rugs, and a slightly-opened bottom window. The place reeked of money-spawned comfort and I wondered who Zacuto had held up to become so well-fixed. Maybe Zacuto might be good for a few hundred bucks as reparations for the harm he'd done, as a gift.

Only one drawback. The damned office was empty.

The nearest precinct sent two detectives over.

"Mr. Zacuto probably went out and he'll be back in no time," the older detective said finally.

Not true. Zacuto didn't come back at all. An All-Points Bulletin was eventually put out for him. As for Teck, I couldn't mention him because I'd have to tell what brought him to Zacuto's in the first place and that was sure as hell going to prove I was an accomplice before the fact.

Anybody who knows about police bureaucrats can tell you what happened next, but here are a few of the grisly details. I made an official statement, which resulted in my being vigorously questioned several times as I had a motive for getting rid of Zacuto and my attempts at putting up an alibi, as it was called, was rated clumsy, even pitiful. The plainclothes detectives union spokesman leaped to my defense, causing me to be deep-sixed from the department two days later. Proceedings were started to get my job back.

While all this was going on, Inga phoned to let me know that she was ditching me. She appreciated that I had done "it," presumably killing Zacuto, to help her, but she didn't want to marry an impulse-driven fellow who couldn't make a living any more. I appreciated the last part of what she said, of course, from her point of view.

And it was no consolation that what had gone wrong was at least partly my fault because I'd *wanted* a double pay-off from Zacuto and Teck. And how was I supposed to know in advance that Teck's way of returning a favor meant getting rid of Zacuto for keeps and burying him someplace? Did you ever hear tell about another guy who would do something like that?

Greed alone, if you ask me, had been my ruination.

While the legal proceedings to get my job back were dragging on, I got work at private detective outfits, at a liquor store and as a night watchman. I can't remember what else.

I didn't get my job back, though, and had to learn

computer programming, which offered no chances for financial profits on the side. What it did offer was a terrible case of carpal tunnel syndrome. Plus which, my rear end was numb as a rule.

One night after work, I took a wrong turn past Cuthbert Street as I walked back. I happened to be near what had once been my favorite watering hole, the dim-lit Twelve Steps to the Bar on Commerce Street. In a what-the-hell mood and having saved enough for one drink, I walked in. Standing at the bar, of course, I ordered a scotch straight up.

One of the customers came over to talk, a friendly character I had known in my other life. He asked me how the detective business was coming along. Sympathy spread over his normally vacant features when I told him the high points of my story.

"A damn shame," he said. "Well, let me buy you a drink and make up for something at least."

This was a perfect chance to accept his drink and then claim I had to be elsewhere right away, so I wouldn't have to pay for a drink for him along with my own.

"No," I said sharply. "I don't want favors. I won't take advantage of people, no more. Just you keep away from me, hear/"

I had decided on the spot that I wouldn't pave the way for fresh disasters by taking freebies, taking something for nothing in sneaky little side deals. Upright and honorable from now on, that was me.

And I was so fanatical about it I kept the solemn

promise to myself. If you really want to know, I kept it for the best part of three full months.

SCOTT FREE

Scott was tagged almost as soon as he hurried into the outsized noisy room. He had expected to lose himself among the others, but one of the burly guys from the senior dance committee suddenly gripped him by an elbow.

"Scottie, you swore you'd come in early and help collect the admissions." It was possible to hear that much over the good rock stuff going full-blast.

"I couldn't find my suit jacket right away." That was the first lie to jump into his head.

"Why didn't you call here instead of leaving us up in the air after you'd impressed everybody by volunteering?"

Actually he had decided against being the one in charge of the money. He smiled easily, as always, when somebody made an accusation against him, and trotted out some moldy little gag to brush off more complaints. "Won't happen next year."

The only response was a sour smile, and it crossed Scott's mind to say that he'd go out to collect admission money in a little while, but he kept quiet. Enough complaining for one night, as far as he was concerned.

He walked halfway across the room, smiling and nodding at some of the guys. As for the girls he saw in those first minutes, they were either used-to-be's or didn't-want-to-know-betters. He smiled at everybody with that same universal blank-faced amiability.

One girl *was* new to him. He supposed that a beauty like her, she must have transferred to Bathhurst High because her folks had to move here. That was some other town's mistake. Those people ought to have kept her by force.

Just as he was on his way over to ask for a dance, the rock band made up of fellow students, and which called itself The Heartbreak of Psoriasis, stopped and went into their intermission mode. The silence would have been a little scary to some of the competition, but Scott always made out well with girls and he grinned before sitting down next to her. Only a few minutes later, he had a Saturday night date.

One of the committee guys happened to be staring at him. Scott stood up, excused himself to the girl because, he said, he had to go out to the lobby and collect admission money. He had promised, he said virtuously, to take on that responsibility.

In the lobby he shrugged, told the expectant guy back of the desk that he was going to the washroom before he did anything else. He did go in, but a little later he "just happened" to leave by the side exit. Rather than face stares like spears at the damn dance, he went home and spent a couple of hours dealing happily with strangers on the Internet.

Scott's dad had bought a car for Scott's stepmother, but Scott used it to go out at night. Dad always warned him to be careful, pointing out that nobody except Scott was responsible for his safety behind the wheel. Dad never liked to drive, a feeling his son shared, but both knew how necessary it was. It had become almost a point of pride for him that he and Dad were different in every way, but when it came to the responsibilities of driving, father and son were like the same edgy human being.

Taking out a good-looking girl like this one was kicky. Alicia was a radiant blonde whose hair flowed in mock carelessness. Her skin was pearly white, her eyes sky blue. She was like an inventory of cheerful colors. Was there a better-looking girl at Bathhurst High? No way.

The usual Saturday night place for him and his friends was Spanky's a diner as bright as a coal mine and located on Route 101. As soon as one of the nerds asked what everybody would be doing after graduation, Scott moved away with Alicia. The in-close dancing they did was enough to convince him that he'd have a great time when he got her alone.

It didn't take long to get her away. Scott only had to tell the guys and their girls smoothly that Alicia had to get home early because she and her people would be having a busy day tomorrow. Alicia didn't contradict him.

He took her by a different route than the one they had come by, driving out to Planters Point. Darkened cars parked out of sight and at a distance from each other, everybody wanting to get lucky and not be interrupted. Scott never knew what he might have done with his girlfriends, if Planters Point didn't offer such safety in numbers.

Alicia had been expecting it, and smilingly waited to embrace him as soon as he turned down the head-lights and leaned back. If he wasn't at home base after a while, he certainly felt sure he was rounding second and running good.

Which was when he heard a noise he couldn't iden-tify right away. He thought his ears were pounding so much it was part of his excitement. No, somebody was calling out loudly and angrily.

Worried about any possible trouble, Scott forced himself to look away and turn, if only briefly, to the left. The moon was bright enough to show him a nearby car with a door open and a sturdy man with a facial tic, his feet apart as he stood in front of that door. The man's fury was almost a disguise, making it impossible to know for sure if he was familiar, but Scott felt thank-fully it was somebody he'd never run across.

He wouldn't give that vicious-looking creep a chance to make out his own features in the moonlight. He ducked so that his body was squeezed down on the floor, the top of his head at just about seat level. He didn't know if he'd been quick enough.

Alicia stared down, her pretty lips forming the words, "What's wrong?" She heard no answer, and ducked in turn, facing him.

That was when a pistol shot thundered in the night air.

Scott saw her mouth opening to scream. Urgently he drew a palm over her lips, applying more pressure than he wanted because she kept struggling to get away from him so she could call out, at least to raise herself and see the murderer. She made a cat-noise to indicate that being forced to stay in place was a source of pin. He withdrew the hand that had been anchoring her, but she stayed in place rather than let herself in for a possible mauling. They glared silently at each other.

Scott was first to hear the sound of a car driving off. Common sense told him which car had moved out. Very soon now his Beetle, too, would be making tracks rather than keeping him in place to be questioned by police wanting definite information.

He raised himself, making sure the other car was gone and nobody was in sight to see them. Again, he seemed to be lucky.

Alicia, too, raised herself. Her eyes swept the area.

"That car was gone before I could even try and get a license number," he said. To himself he thanked God. To her he added, "At least I saved—saved *you*—from any possible trouble."

"Did you see what make of car it was?" she prodded.

"Too dark for that, too." It almost rattled him to say anything that was absolutely true.

"Have you got a cellular in the car? Someone has to report it to the police."

"No phone. Somebody else will report it, I'm sure,

and your people won't know you were her." He considered. "We don't *really* know what happened. It could have been just a flat tire, now that I think of it."

"You have to assume it was a murder."

"It could have been, sure, but when a body turns up the case will be solved. If there *is* a case, like I say."

"Suppose the body has been taken away so it can be buried in secret, then it might never be found."

Sensible as he was sounding when he tried to convince her that nothing needed to be done by them, Alicia didn't calm down until he had repeated the same idea any number of times. Besides, she hadn't seen anything crucial, either. Whatever she herself might tell the police would be useless to them.

To impress her he said firmly that if there was no report about the Planters Point disturbance by tomorrow night—make that tomorrow afternoon, he contradicted himself when she looked disapproving— he'd get in touch with the police without giving her name. As a good citizen, of course, he'd put himself forward if it came to that. He promised.

Dad made a point of turning the radio news up loud every morning and talking to Scott's stepmother until the weather forecast came on. Then he'd listen almost prayerfully. Scott always used the lull to sneak a third cup of coffee and swear it was his second if he happened to get caught.

He listened intently to the newscast on this particular morning. It seemed that there had been anonymous phone calls by several people claiming that a pistol shot had been fired last night at Planters Point. No spent bullet had been found, and no gun either. (It stood to reason that there was no sign of a corpse and no record of somebody with a bullet wound.) The Police Department had issued a stern statement against practical jokers wasting the time of hard-working guardians of law and order.

Scott was looking out for the sight of Alicia Diamond from the minute he got to school. Even if she wasn't candy for the eyes, Scott wouldn't have missed talking to her. He got his chance between classes, stopping Alicia on the way to study hall.

"I phoned the police this morning, like I promised. They've had other calls and they think the whole business is a practical joke."

"Did you give your name like you said you would?"

"Sure, but I don't think the cop I talked to even bothered to write it down. If that's good enough for him, it ought to be good enough for us. We can forget the whole thing before they do."

"Maybe we should *both* talk to them."

He was suddenly tired of having to remind her that nobody could prove that anything had actually happened. "Tell you what, 'licia. Meet me tonight at half-past eight and we'll call the police together from Zero's."

Zero's was a convenience store near the Southern tip of Bathhurst, an arm-long place with old-fashioned phone booths from grandma's day, insuring privacy to those who wanted or needed it.

"You can hear me call," he said, looking forward to fitting himself into the same booth with her. "And you can talk if you want to, confirming what I say."

"Of course I'll talk to whoever answers."

"And after we get through, it'll be dead easy to look at the town again from Planters Point."

"We'll see about that," Alicia said diplomatically.

He buttonholed Chris Owen on the way out of school, quietly explaining in the fewest words that he'd phone Chris on his own line at exactly nine-fifteen, and that Chris would identify himself as a member of the police department. All that Scott's best buddy at school had to do after that was to listen and say that a record of the call had been made and that the department would get in touch if there was any need.

Feeling set up, Scott went home. His stepmother must have got gas for the Beetle earlier, so he asked for another loan tonight. He said he'd be doing his assignment this afternoon, and went upstairs to call the two nerds from English and science for the answers they'd know without diving into books or software. He decided to stay in the room a little longer to make everything look good and put some rock music on the radio, making it low enough to be able to tell his stepmother later that he hadn't heard anything and it must've come from a neighboring house. He was still humming *I Want to Make Love to You One More Time* when the music stopped and a five-minute newscast came on.

A young woman's murdered body had been discovered just off Route 101, the newscaster said with ghoulish pleasure. Ramona Thurston, twenty-seven, a computer technician by trade, had been shot somewhere else with a .32 pistol and the body dumped in a ditch.

With something solid to work on, the police had gone at it. A man named Karl Willock, who lived eighty miles off in the town of Garton, had been engaged to Ramona Thurston until a recent quarrel split them up. He was being question, and more information was expected soon.

Scott took Alicia to Zero's convenience store on that chilly night and went through the ritual of talking to the "police," actually to his buddy, Chris, as arranged. Alicia gave her name and seemed grim, but calmer.

"I don't' want to see Planters Point so soon after what happened last night," she said when they were back in the car and he was starting there by the long way around.

"We could 'rest up' for a few minutes...."

He liked to make that sort of remark so that the girl he was with could say snappily that it wouldn't be "restful." She might think of herself as being witty, even while her resistance to the idea was being lowered.

This stubborn girl was different, however. "I mean it, Scott. Please take me straight home."

He made a point of letting her see him smile regretfully, but told himself he'd never go near her again. If a dude took the trouble to do what some girl wanted, he shouldn't get hung up afterwards.

Scott arrived home in time to join Dad and a gleaming half-empty bottle of Heineken's along with a foggy glass for the end of the Jets game on the tube. Dad was filling him in on some of the highlights of the Jets' glorious victory when a teaser came on for the news broadcast that was going to follow.

"The police have made an arrest in last night's murder, which probably happened at Planters Point. Stay tuned for...."

"Mind if I watch just a few minutes of the news?"

"Up to you," Dad said, maneuvering the beer bottle in one hand while brushing cracker crumbs onto a napkin. "Just let me know if it's going to rain tomorrow...."

He nodded and watched the pictures of Karl Willock under restraint, learning only that no confession had been made, but the police spokesman was confident that "the perpetrator had been apprehended by self-less work from members of the Bathhurst Police Department."

It slipped Scott's mind to wait around for the weather, but he went into the kitchen and told Dad that tomorrow, like today, was going to be very windy. At least, he added, that's what the newsman had said.

Not till Scott was on the way upstairs for at least half an hour on the Net did it occur to him that there was something wrong with the pictures he had seen on the tube, those pictures of Willock. He didn't want to think about it and pin down anything that might be disturbing, but his mind insisted he try his best.

He wasn't used to having his mind push him around, but couldn't make himself think about some different subject.

He was too upset to go near the Net tonight. As soon as he took his clothes off, he started for the shower to calm himself, but ended up taking a hot bath. By the time his head finally hit the pillow, the whole mess was back on his mind.

He'd go over it just once again before shutting his eyes and corking off. Just once.

This guy Karl Willock was the major suspect for having committed the murder last night and hauling the girl's body away from Planters Point. Okay, so far.

Scott must have seen the murderer last night, a furious-looking guy with a facial tic. One eye constantly went shut unavoidably and the corresponding corners of his lips soared as if to meet it.

But—

Willock had been shown close-up on the tube, being led some place by a police officer. The camera had been on Willock for a minute at least, long enough to make anybody jumpy, even if there was nothing physically wrong with him. No facial tic. None.

And it meant—didn't it?—that *the cops had arrested the wrong man!* An innocent guy was likely to be tried for murder, an accused man with no facial tic!

The way to keep that from going down was for him, Scott Finley, the one witness, to come forward and tell what he knew, for Scott to finally put himself ini the frying pan.

What with one thing and another, Scott didn't get much sleep that night.

He woke up next morning, convinced he'd had a nightmare. But a still photograph of the dark-haired, dry-eyed Carl Willock appeared on Page One of the *Bathhurst Vigilant*, and it reminded him all over again about everything that had happened.

By the time he got to the school for a day's learning, he had decided to write an anonymous note to the police and tell what he'd seen that proved Willock wasn't the man they were after.

He was feeling proud of himself for wanting to do his civic duty, even if anonymously, until he remembered that the police had whined about anonymous phone calls when the case first broke. No unsigned letter would be taken seriously.

His buddy Chris Owen wasn't anywhere in sight. He finally turned up in the school cafeteria during early lunch period. His eyes roved from side to side, looking away in hopes of finding somebody else.

"Alicia gets a late lunch period, but I thought she might be able to come here this time," he explained, not that Scott had asked. "Great girl, that 'licia is. Wonderful. If she happens to be yours, just tell me and I'll go no further."

"Take her for Christmas," Scott said, knowing he wouldn't get any information out of Chris until this subject was exhausted. "I'm always unselfish. How'd you meet her?"

""Well, after you played that joke on her last night

about calling the police department and me answering, it struck me that she's got a sweet voice. I hunted her up this morning before home room class, and we seem to like each other."

"You haven't told Alicia about that phone call, have you?"

"No, of course not. She'd never talk to me again. As it is I'll save her the anguish and be unselfish, too."

"Have you mentioned it to anybody else?" He had emphasized the need for secrecy at the time Chris agreed to do it, but there was no harm hammering the point across.

"No, it might get back to 'licia if I did, but I tell you this much, good buddy: you're lucky as hell that the cops caught the right guy so our consciences won't bother us."

"*My* conscience, that's right."

He was calmer afterwards, but the big trouble remained under his nose. Just the same he told himself that he hadn't necessarily seen the killer, although he'd certainly somebody who wasn't Willock.

Common sense came to his rescue one more time: if Willock was innocent, there'd be no evidence against him and he'd be set free. Scott's best course of action was the one he wanted to take: forget about it instead of making some unholy show of himself. He'd been on the right track all along.

Scott looked at the newspaper when preliminaries of Karl Willock's trial got under way. Nothing much seemed to happen, though, so he gave up on it. After all, he was always being told to get a life and he kept busy at it.

He saw Alicia in school or at a dance every so often, and smiled agreeably at her as he did at all his other used-to-be girls. Alicia either smiled back hesitantly or waved in acknowledgment, but didn't try to talk to him. Scott never felt offended by that. As far as she was concerned, all he wanted was to disappear into the crowd.

Chris was nearly always in her company. They giggled together as if at some private joke, which Chris never told him about. It was impossible to figure what made Chris choose one girl when the school was full of them. There would be plenty of time to pick out one and not be able to get away from her. Chris was called Ork by his friends and he seemed like an ork if there ever was one.

The Willock trial was getting under way, and Scott went so far as to write an anonymous letter addressed to the chief defense lawyer and one to the district attorney's assistant who was handling the prosecution's case. He had already put stamps on both letters before deciding they could only get him in trouble and ripping them to shreds instead. What he had to do was to keep a few words in his head all the time: if Willock is innocent, he'll walk.

Every once in a while the gang at Spanky's Diner would center down on the trial. Scott never hung in for that stuff if Alicia and Chris were on the scene, but he listened more than usual if they weren't. The prosecution claimed that Willock didn't have any alibi for the night, saying he'd been home alone.

Willock, testifying in his own behalf, said that Ramona Thurston had admitted to him that she had acquired another boyfriend and said she enjoyed having two dudes on her string. All that the enraged Willock knew about the other guy was that he had pressed her to marry him and that he had a very secure job, a safe job he was unlikely to ever lose.

On April Fool's Day, which seemed like a grisly coincidence, the case went to the jury and Scott came down with a miserable headache that nothing seemed to fix. People talked about the deliberations because the jury stayed out for five whole days, and everybody felt that the member like getting food for free and staying away from their jobs. Scott didn't tell anybody how much he sympathized with them for not wanting to make a definite choice. He'd been tested with a G.I. series after that damned long headache, and it was hard to keep feelings to himself rather than cause discussion among pals. He spent time seeing a lot of movies, even a few "chick flicks" with new dates, and listening to his music. Most of all he planted himself on the Net, where he never gave his real name.

Karl Willock was found guilty.

The judge, agreeing with the protesting defense attorney that the evidence had been circumstantial in the main—"though not entirely inadequate for that"—salted Willock away for seven to fifteen years. With good behavior, he might be free again in five-and-a-half.

That was that. A verdict had been given by jurors who'd spent a lot more time figuring the ins and outs of the case than Scott Finley had. He'd been a damn fool to take the whole business so seriously at the start, but everything was settled now.

One news story that he read after sentencing was enough to confirm his appreciation of his own good sense. The police were now able to make it public that Willock had been strongly suspected in a number of criminal cases, but there had never been enough evidence to bring him to trial. The police felt sure he had committed half a hundred burglaries, at least. The Garton police had questioned the man, but set him free every time. If anything could have cheered Scott further, the news that Willock was almost certainly a habitual criminal who had never served time was just the right ticket.

It proved even more definitely that he had been right all the time in not sticking in his neck out as far as the murder was involved. He didn't like to think of it so baldly, but he knew he had got away with doing what he wanted.

The next hurdle for him, a different matter altogether, was graduation at school. It was supposed to be a sad-happy time for everybody, but Scott wanted nothing more than to get it over and move on to college. He hoped he'd never have to come back to the town where he had lived for almost eighteen years, where he was known by everyone. He had been accepted at nearby

Garton College, choosing it because it cost no more than Dad was able to afford. If he did well, he hoped he'd be able to go to Law School at Columbia in New York City on a scholarship and be much further away from his home town.

His pal, Chris, had expected to join him, but Alicia's new importance in his life had caused him to enroll with her in college at Austin in Texas. Scott and Chris shook hands vigorously after the graduation ceremonies and promised to talk on the Net and see each other when holiday leave rolled around. Scott sounded sincere when he agreed instead of saying that he hoped to be elsewhere at that time. He wouldn't have called it selfish.

As for Alicia, Scott kissed the radiant blonde beauty on a cheek and wished her the best. She smiled back at him and offered good wishes in return while adding that they'd all keep in touch. It was like they had been nothing more than casual friends, as if they weren't the keepers of a nasty and bitter secret of which even she only knew a part.

The night's party was a downer. Every girl he saw reminded him of something in the past. The guys wanted to talk about what one of them actually called "old times."

He quit the place with several couples going out to Spanky's, and joined them. The talk turned to another session of warmed-over memories, so he went home and on to the Net. He didn't go to sleep until ten o'clock the next morning.

He had visited Garton College a couple of times, but he was not sure where to take Dad in helping him to move in. Scott's roommate didn't know him, either; he had quickly passed up the chance to room with a guy who had graduated with him. After the physical work was done, Dad stayed around to see the place. Scott could hardly wait for him to leave so that he'd have seen the last of him, and of Bathhurst, the end of his past.

Scott Finley was free.

He made a point of checking out some girls and was pleased by what he saw. A few guys told him about the best eating places, the bars, the bargains; and the local characters, of whom there seemed to be plenty. One senior kept a horse stabled nearby, for instance, and rode it around campus at night. A tenured professor collected paintings in which green was the primary color. Mr. Hammond, the instructor who gave the orientation lectures, had for some unknown reason stopped taking passengers in his two-year-old car.

But by the time the first of three orientation lectures was due, Scott was feeling comfortable in these surroundings. He was going to enjoy college and had never begrudged working hard. After all he'd been through during the last several month, he felt he was entitled to enjoy himself—to please himself.

The orientation instructor turned out to be a dark-haired flushed-faced man in his late thirties, not particularly at ease. As if to spare him, Scott looked away while listening, and looked, instead, at the questioners who asked what anybody genuinely interested in college should have found out a while ago.

He didn't see Mr. Hammond again until the next night, as he was coming back to his room after a date with the prettiest girl around. Hammond was walking towards him from the opposite direction and Scott had a chance to take a long look at him. He was about to offer a greeting when he noticed the man's left eye close briefly and the corresponding corners of his lips moved upward. Mr. Hammond was one of those guys with a facial tic, just like—

Just like—

He remembered the car into which Hammond would allow nobody during the last months. It might be that there were unmistakable dried stains all over the front passenger seat, stains that he didn't want anyone to see and identify. Bloodstains, of course.

Hammond, whose flushed features gave him a look of perpetual fury, was the Garton resident who had killed Ramona Thurston. One eye opened and closed furiously, a nervous motion that Scott well remembered.

"You," Hammond whispered, swiftly moving so that he was in front of the suddenly frightened Scott. "You're the one I saw. I'd know that scared look anyplace."

The man's hard hands came up to circle Scott's neck. For the last time in his life Scott tried to avoid consequences, this time by pulling away, but all he saw was those hating eyes, all he felt was....

The only witness to the crime happened to be Chris Owen, who had come to Garton in hopes of personally clearing up paper work relating to his transfer to Austin in Texas. He'd also planned to surprise Scott with a quick visit, but didn't located him until too late. He didn't hesitate to turn away immediately, sensing that Scott's life was over and knowing that his future plans would be delayed indefinitely if he stayed to testify against the squint-eyed murderer. Scott had convinced him over the years that a dude had to look out for himself, to be unselfish toward himself. Chris Owen had learned that lesson very well indeed.

ACKNOWLEDGMENTS

"The Battered Bride" by "Norman Hunt" was originally published in *The Man from U.N.C.L.E. Magazine*, October 1966. Copyright © 1966 by Leo Margulies Publications; Copyright © 2013 by Morris Hershman.

"Charlotte's Ruse" by Morris Hershman was originally published in *101 Sneaky Little Sleuth Stories*, edited by Robert Weinberg, Stefan Dziemianowicz, and Martin H. Greenberg, Barnes & Noble Books, 1997. Copyright © 1997, 2013 by Morris Hershman.

"Chicken Contest" by Morris Hershman was originally published in *Mike Shayne Mystery Magazine*, November 1964. Copyright © 1964 by Renown Publications; Copyright © 2013 by Morris Hershman.

"The Devil's Payoff" by "Norman Hunt" was originally published in *Mike Shayne Mystery Magazine*, February 1965. Copyright © 1965 by Renown Publications; Copyright © 2013 by Morris Hershman.

"A Knife for My Love" by "Arnold English" was originally published in *Guilty Detective Stories Magazine*, September 1957. Copyright © 1957 by Crestwood Publications; Copyright © 2013 by Morris Hershman.

ABOUT THE AUTHOR

MORRIS HERSHMAN is the author of some ninety novels, including mysteries, science fiction, romances, gothics, and many others, a number of which are being published or reprinted by the Borgo Press. He lives and works in New York.